To Henrietta and Rosemary,
both of whom have helped me so much
MN

For all the children and teachers
at Lilliesleaf Primary School
PB

BLOOMSBURY
CHILDREN'S
BOOKS

First published in Great Britain in 2002 by Bloomsbury Publishing Plc
38 Soho Square, London, W1D 3HB

Text copyright © Marjorie Newman 2002
Illustrations copyright © Patrick Benson 2002
The moral right of the author and illustrator has been asserted

A CIP catalogue record of this book is available from the British Library
ISBN 0 7475 5883 3

Designed by Sarah Hodder

Printed in Hong Kong/China

1 3 5 7 9 10 8 6 4 2

Mole and
the Baby Bird

by Marjorie Newman

illustrated by

Patrick Benson

BLOOMSBURY
CHILDREN'S
BOOKS

Mole found a baby bird. It had fallen out of its nest.

Mole waited and waited but no big bird came to help it,

so Mole took the
baby bird home.

He made a nest for it.
"Look, Mum!" he said.

"It's very, very hard to take care of a baby bird," said Mum.

"They usually die," said Dad.

"My bird won't die," said Mole.

His friends helped him find food for the baby.

Mum showed him how to feed it.

Mole fed it whenever it chirped.
And the bird didn't die. It grew!

"It's my pet bird," said Mole.
"It's not a pet bird. It's a wild bird," said Mum.
The bird fluttered its wings.

"Your bird is trying to fly," said Mum.
"No!" cried Mole. "It mustn't fly!"

Mole found some wood and some nails.

He borrowed Dad's toolbox.

"What are you making?"
asked Dad.

"I'm making a cage for my pet bird," said Mole.

"It's not a pet bird.
  It's a wild bird," said Dad.
"You should let it fly."

"No!" cried Mole.

He put his bird into its new cage.
The bird was sad.

Mum was sad, too.
But Mole kept his bird, because he loved it.

Then Grandad came to visit.
He looked at Mole's pet bird.

Presently Grandad said,
"Let's go for a walk, little Mole."

Grandad took Mole to the top of a high hill.

Mole looked down at the trees far below.

He felt the wild wind trying to lift him.

"Wheee! I'm flying!" cried Mole.
"Nearly," said Grandad.

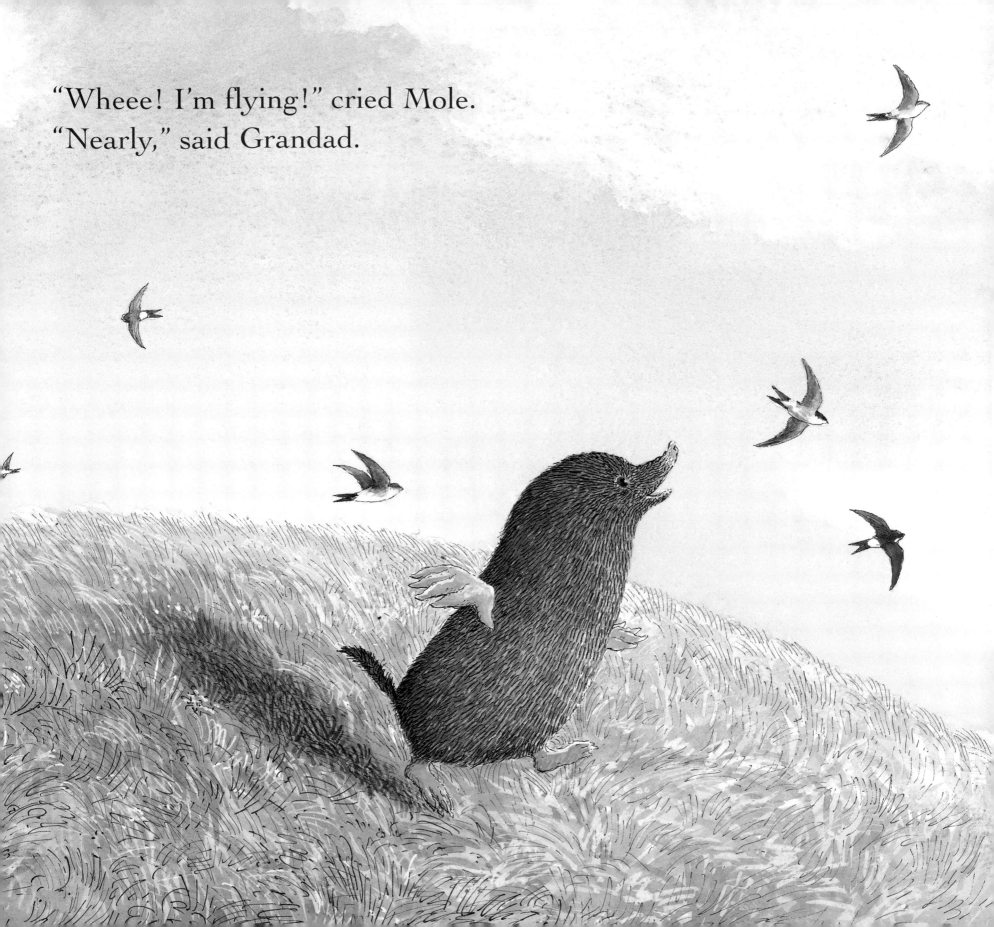

When Mole got home he looked at his bird.

It was sitting very still in its cage
in Mole's dark underground room.

"Birds are meant to fly," said Mole.

He opened the cage door and he let his bird fly away,
because he loved it.
Then he cried.

Next day Mole went into the forest.
He saw his bird flying, soaring, free.
And Mole was glad.